Colliding

with Chris

Dan Harder
Illustrated by Kevin O'Malley

Hyperion Books for Children

NEW YORK

Text © 1997 by Dan Harder.
Illustrations © 1997 by Kevin O'Malley.

Printed in Singapore.

First Edition
1 3 5 7 9 10 8 6 4 2

Designed by Stephanie Bart-Horvath

Library of Congress Cataloging-in-Publication Data
Harder, Dan (Dan Wymbs)
Colliding with Chris / by Dan Harder ; illustrated by Kevin O'Malley
p.   cm.
Summary: A young boy's first ride on a bicycle with hand brakes turns out
to be much wilder than he ever imagined.
ISBN 0-7868-0125-5 (trade)—ISBN 0-7868-2098-5 (lib. bdg.)
[1. Bicycles and bicycling—Fiction.] I. O'Malley, Kevin, 1961-
ill. II. Title
PZ7.H21735Co   1997
[E]—dc20
96-14738

The artwork for each picture is prepared using a combination of oil
paints, colored pencils, and design markers.

The text for this book is set in 17–point Missive.

To Ora, Boo, and Number Nine I dedicate each bouncing line
—D. H.

For Danny—oops! I mean Brendan
—K. O.

Are you sure you can ride?" his grandfather asked

as Christopher climbed on his shiny new bike.

"Sure!" yelled Chris as he lifted

his feet and started to roll down the hill.

There was **no** need to worry, **no**

need for concern. He would pedal to start

and pedal to slow and that was as much as

he needed to know.

And so as he rolled toward the roses below he was **sure** he'd be able to stop. What a look of **surprise** you could see in his eyes when the pedals didn't respond.

"**Watch out!**" he cried as he started to ride toward his grandmother pruning a rose.

He avoided the branches, avoided the thorns, and barely avoided his grandmother, too, but he couldn't avoid so he didn't avoid all the **roses** she threw in the air.

As fast as he came, as quickly he went—right through the roses and into a shed. He missed all the shovels and missed all the pots but a **spider** was spinning in just the wrong spot.

So out of the garden and out of the shed, the
spider, the roses,
and Christopher sped.

The bicycle rattled and clattered and clanged
as Christopher rode from the shed to the woods.

He ducked under branches and skirted a stump, but
bumped the rump of a grumbling **bear.**

As it is with a feather, so it is with a bear, when
it isn't supported, it falls from the air to land on what-
ever is passing below—like a boy on a bike that is
out of control.

Between the trees and toward a stream went the wobbling runaway bike—between the trees and into a stream and straight toward a rather large **trout.**

Out of his wits and out of the water and **into the air** leapt the rather large trout—out of his wits and out of the water and onto the **bear's** inhospitable snout!

Faster and farther they helplessly sped, out of the forest and onto a farm. They avoided a cow and cut through the corn and bounced over cabbage and onions and beans, but they couldn't avoid so they didn't avoid going right through the pen of a pig.

With a **pig** in his lap and a **bear** on his back, not to mention the **spider**, the **roses**, and **trout**, he looked like a clown as he sped into town on the day of the big parade. **"Look out!"** cried Chris as he cut through the crowd and headed right into a **band.**

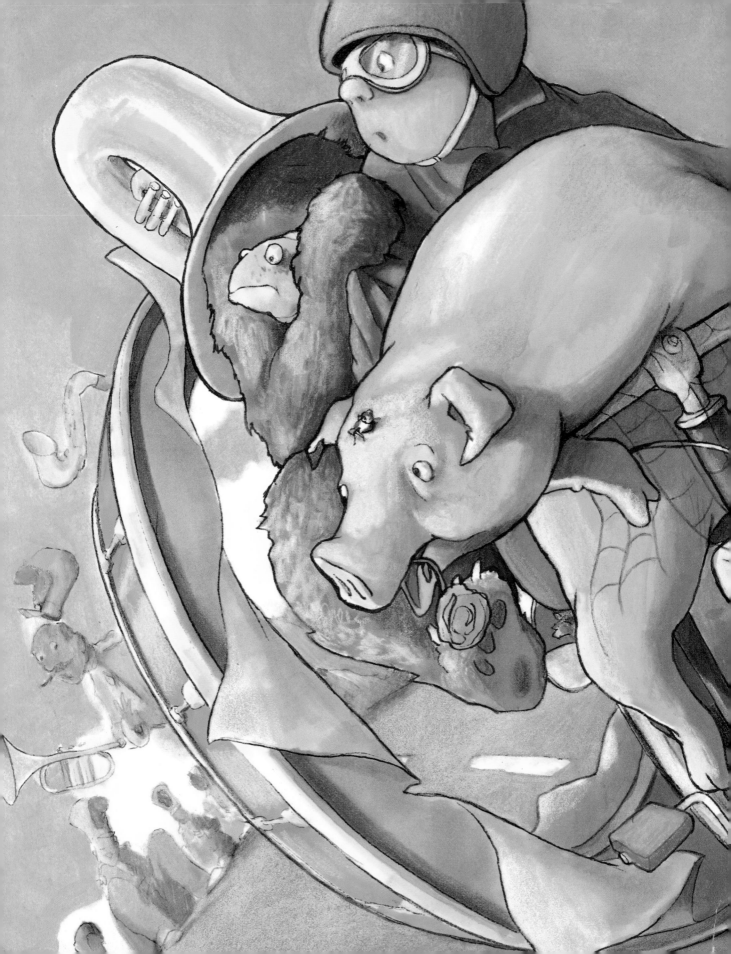

He **CRASHED** through the drums and squealed through the flutes then *BLASTED* smack into the horns. A trumpet went right, a bugle went left, and a tuba flew into the air. Flashing and twirling, it spun as it fell to land on the head of the bear.

They oinked and they roared, they wriggled and steered, but nothing they did slowed that bicycle down, till it jostled and joggled and jumped from a bump to land in some hay at the back of a truck.

Then out of the town, past the farm, and through the forest of trees, the truck rumbled up to the top of the hill where Christopher's ride had begun.

"**Hold on!**" yelled Chris as the truck took a turn and the bicycle started to slide.

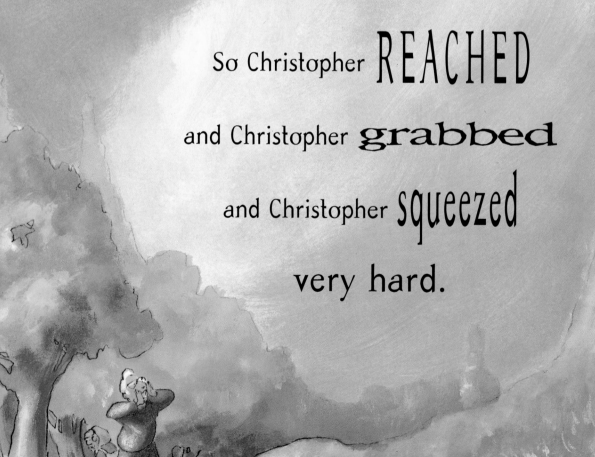

His grandparents, meanwhile, had run to the shed to follow the tracks and see where they led. But just as they started to enter the woods, what did they see at the crest of the hill? A **boy** with a **bear**, a **pig**, and a **trout**, some **roses**, a **tuba**, a **spider and web**, all of them crowded on top of a bike on a ride that seemed never to end.

His grandfather guessed what was causing the trouble and shouted to Chris up above. "The brakes aren't near your feet, my boy. The brakes are near your hands!"

So Christopher REACHED

and Christopher **grabbed**

and Christopher squeezed

very hard.

When something is speeding, then comes to a stop, it's liable to fly if it's riding on top.

Off went the **tuba**, the **trout**, and the **bear**, the **spider**, the **roses**, the **pig** in the air . . .

. . . the **tuba** to town, the **pig** to its pen, the **trout** to the stream, the **bear** to the woods, the **spider and web** to a doorway and sill, and the **roses** to scatter all over the ground.

And where was the boy who had started to roll before he was sure how to stop? There in the dirt, though not really hurt, by the side of his muddy new bike.

"You had quite a ride," his grandfather said.

"You ready to try it again?"

"OH, SURE," said Chris with the hint of a smile, "though I think that I'll rest for a while."